TAS AND BEC ARE GOING DOWN THE ROAD

97

KNOWLEDGE BOOKS

MASTERY DECODABLES

Gem knows Tas and Bec were in the main street.

Gem knows the main street ran by a farm.

Gem knows the farm had a steel gate.

Gem knows Brin could see Tas and Bec.

4

Gem knows Brin lives on the farm.

What did Tas do?

Tas went out of the garden with Bec.

Tas ran down the long road.

Bec flew down the long road.

Tas and Bec saw the steel gate.

Oh no! The gate was open.

Tas and Bec went into the farm garden.

Tas could see the small tail of a farm animal.

What is it?

It is a sheep.

Oh no! Tas and Bec are afraid.

The sheep can eat grain from a bin.

The sheep is big.

Look! Brin is with the sheep.

Tas and Bec are not afraid now.